Advice

from a

Very Large Toad!

Written and Illustrated
by

Daryl B. Enos

AmCole Enterprises, Inc.
P.O. Box 41
Young Harris, GA 30582
JKBishop@yhc.edu   FAX 706-896-1846
          706-896-5147

As I was leaving my house on my way to a costume party, I was stopped by a very large toad.

"Kati," said the toad, "before you go to the costume party, allow me to offer you some advice."

"If you should happen
upon an old woman with
a broken broom, don't
offer to fix it for her."

"Why not," I asked.

"Because she's a witch,"
said the toad.

"Oh my!" said I, "Will
she turn me into a frog?"

"Don't be silly," said
the toad. "When her
broom is fixed, she'll
take you for a
test ride."

"Oh no! You should
never accept a ride
from a stranger,"
I said.

"So true, so true," said
the toad. "But even if
you do, you're
not in trouble... yet."

"You will land on a large bat that is flying close to the ground. Your fall will be broken by the bat, but the bat will fly into a tree. The bat, of course, is a vampire and he will be quite upset."

"And he'll bite me on the neck and I'll turn into a frog?" I asked.

"No, Kati" said the toad, "his fangs were knocked so loose he'll be afraid to bite ice cream."

He's upset because his head hurts. You're not in trouble yet, but whatever you do, don't put a bandage on him."

"Well, I'd have to help,"
I said. "It's the right
thing to do."

"So true, so true," sighed
the toad. "And when
you do, you will find a
bandage on the ground.
Unknown to you, the
other end is connected to
a mummy."

"As you wrap up the vampire the mummy will unravel. Embarrassed and chilled to the bones, the mummy will be upset."

"Now I know," I said. "The curse of the mummy will turn me into a frog!"

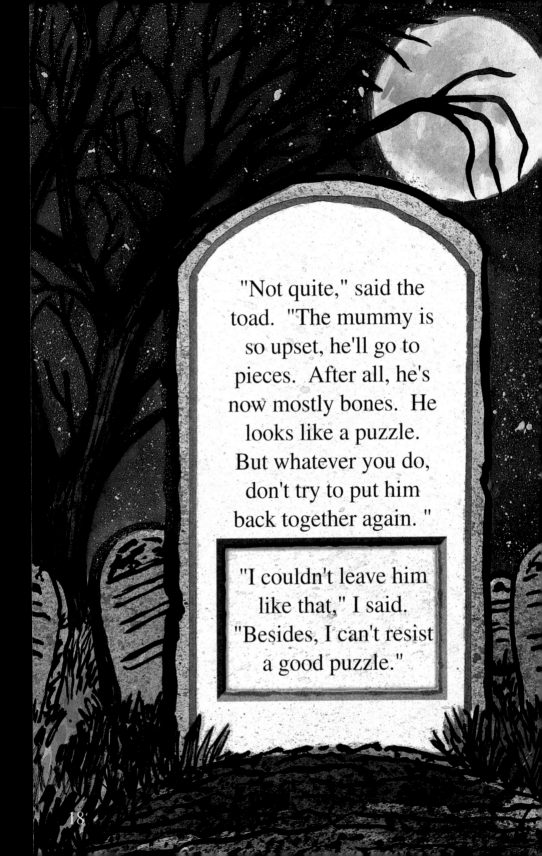

"Not quite," said the toad. "The mummy is so upset, he'll go to pieces. After all, he's now mostly bones. He looks like a puzzle. But whatever you do, don't try to put him back together again. "

"I couldn't leave him like that," I said. "Besides, I can't resist a good puzzle."

The toad continued, "A werewolf will happen along and offer to help. He's willing to lend the mummy his coat. He is also an expert on bones. But when you are done..."

"I'm positive a werewolf can't turn me into a frog," I interrupted.

"No, Kati, no," said the slightly annoyed toad. "You'll be missing one bone. You'll look all around, but it will finally be found in the werewolf's back pocket."

"He'll make an excuse
and admit he couldn't
resist taking the bone.
You'll scold him
anyway. He'll be sad
and upset, but you're
not in trouble... yet.
So, what ever you do,
don't start feeling sorry
for him."

"Oh the poor thing,"
I sighed.

"But you <u>will</u> feel
sorry for him,"
continued the toad.
"And to get his mind
off of the bone, you'll
play fetch with
a stick.

On one very long
throw, the werewolf
will try to catch the
stick without
watching where he
is going."

KEEP OFF THE
GRASS

"He will crash into
the witch! Her broom
will break. Now the
witch will become
very upset. But
you're not
in trouble... yet."

"But, even though she is upset, whatever you do, don't offer to fix it again," said the toad.

"Why?" said I.

"Because this time you <u>will</u> be in trouble," said the toad.

"Now I finally get turned into a frog?" I frantically asked.

"No, Kati," the toad said seriously. "You'll be in trouble because it will be past your bedtime. You'll have to rush home, and you will have missed all the costume party fun."

33

"So when do I get turned into a toad?" asked Kati. "You don't," said the toad. "But isn't that how you became a toad," Kati asked."Heavens no, Kati," chuckled the toad, "I've been a toad all my life."

Next year I'm going to offer my own advice to Nicole.

"If you should happen upon a large, talking toad, and he offers you some advice... you're not in trouble yet! But, whatever you do,

DON'T LISTEN!

But you will, and he will tell you about a witch with a broken broom, and..."